Bella's Big Surprise

Written by Terry Grubbs

Illustrated by Yu-Mei Han

This book is dedicated to our beautiful granddaughter Isabelle.

Grandpa and I have never stopped praying for you!
Love forever, your Grandma

Hi! My name is Bella.

I'm a caterpillar.

I eat a lot.

I eat leaves. They taste yummy.

But if I were a cow I would eat grass,
make milk for babies,
and maybe ice cream too.

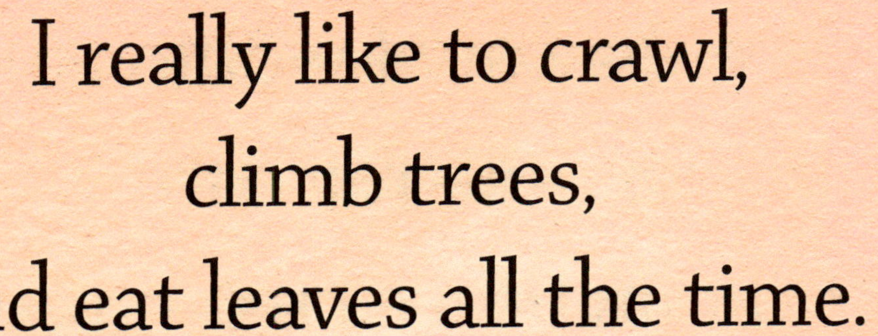

I really like to crawl,
climb trees,
and eat leaves all the time.

But if I were a horse,
I would eat hay.
I would give rides to children,
so they could laugh and have fun.

I eat so much that sometimes
I out grow my skin,

and then I get new skin.

But if I were a duck,
I could eat flies,
and go swimming all day.

I am very sleepy today
and hungry.

But if I were a bear,
I would eat berries and then climb
in a deep dark cave and sleep for months.

Sometimes I wish I could fly, but I'm just
a caterpillar named Bella.

I only eat leaves.
I wonder what honey tastes like.

But if I were a bee,
I could drink from flowers, make honey,
and "FLY!"

I am hungry again today,
and so, so sleepy.
My head is starting to spin.

But if I were a dog,
I would not be sleepy. I would play ball
and run around all day.

Today I became so sleepy,
I made my own bed and climbed in.

Good Night! See you after my nap.

But if I were a sleepy cat,
I would cuddle on someone's lap
and take my nap.

Then I woke up,
and surprise,
GOD had made me into
a big beautiful butterfly.

Now I can "FLY".
He changed my name to Isabelle.
Thank you, GOD.

Letter to the Reader:

I believe God made you special.
He made you exactly who you are supposed to be.
Sometimes we wish we were someone else.
Please remember God has made you special,
with unique qualities that only you have.

God gives us dreams.
Bella wished she could fly,
and then one day she could fly.
So dream big.

God has so many wonderful things ahead just for you.
Sometimes He has a new name He will call you by.
He always has a great plan for your life.

www.ingramcontent.com/pod-product-compliance
Lightning Source LLC
Chambersburg PA
CBHW042145030726
47599CB00002B/626